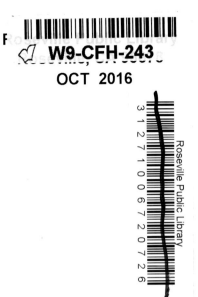

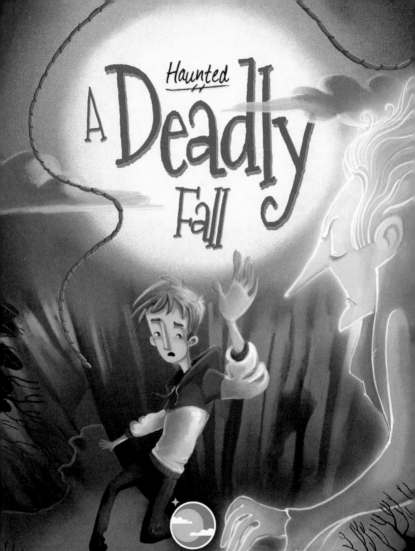

A Deadly Fall

Haunted

Fall

Spellbound

An Imprint of Magic Wagon
abdopublishing.com

By Rich Wallace Illustrated By Daniela Volpari

abdopublishing.com

Published by Magic Wagon, a division of ABDO, PO Box 398166,
Minneapolis, Minnesota 55439. Copyright © 2017 by Abdo
Consulting Group, Inc. International copyrights reserved in all
countries. No part of this book may be reproduced in any form
without written permission from the publisher. Spellbound™ is a
trademark and logo of Magic Wagon.

Printed in the United States of America, North Mankato, Minnesota.
052016
092016

Written by Rich Wallace
Illustrated by Daniela Volpari
Edited by Heidi M.D. Elston
Designed by Laura Mitchell

Library of Congress Cataloging-in-Publication Data

Names: Wallace, Rich, author. | Volpari, Daniela, 1985- illustrator.
Title: A deadly fall / by Rich Wallace ; illustrated by Daniela Volpari.
Description: Minneapolis, MN : Magic Wagon, | 2017 | Series: Haunted |
    Summary: When Stu hears a voice calling him late at night, follows it to the
    haunted house down the road, and sees the ghost of a boy who was murdered
    fifty years before, he feels compelled to find out why the ghost is reaching out to
    him--even if it means risking his own life.
Identifiers: LCCN 2015048142 (print) | LCCN 2015048978 (ebook) | ISBN
    9781624021473 (print) | ISBN 9781680779622 (ebook)
Subjects: LCSH: Ghost stories. | Haunted houses--Juvenile fiction. |
    Murder--Juvenile fiction. | CYAC: Ghosts--Fiction. | Haunted
    houses--Fiction. | Murder--Fiction. | Horror stories.
Classification: LCC PZ7.W15877 De 2016 (print) | LCC PZ7.W15877 (ebook) | DDC
    813.6--dc23
LC record available at http://lccn.loc.gov/2015048142

Table of Contents

Chapter 1
Stuuu

I woke up late one night. An *eerie* voice was calling my name. It wasn't coming from anywhere in our house.

I thought it might be my friend Dan playing a joke. But it didn't sound like Dan. The voice sounded *desperate* and alone. Who else would be calling me?

Stuuunuunununuu

I *sneaked* out of the house and walked down the hill. Dan's house was dark and quiet. The voice was farther down the road. The cry grew weaker. Someone needed **help**

I walked faster. The wind **chilled** my bones, but I was starting to sweat from *FEAR*.

Everyone says the Davidson place

is **HAUNTED**. It's been empty since

long before I was born.

Stuuuuuuuuuu...

I'd never heard a voice from it.

Until tonight. I didn't believe in

ghosts. But lately I'd seen some

strange things around town.

Tonight I felt weird ENERGY inside the Davidson house. It made my skin tingle. I poked around downstairs for a few minutes. The house was quiet. There was no sign of whoever called me.

"Hello?"

I said. My voice

sounded weak and

AFRAID. I tried again. "Hello?"

Maybe I'd find someone upstairs.

Or some *thing*. I took a few timid

steps. But a **SHADOW** on the

stairs stopped me cold!

I got out of there fast. I knew

I'd never get back to sleep

that night!

Chapter 2
Splat

Dan laughed when I told him about the ghost. "There's no such thing, Stu," he said. "But a kid did **DIE** at that house. He fell off the deck."

"It was about sixty years ago," Dan said. "Some say it was an accident, but I don't think so. I think it was *murder*."

"Mark Davidson and his friend Eddie were arguing about something," Dan added. "A girl or money. Who knows. Anyway, Mark CRASHED over the railing."

We stepped onto the creaky deck. The gorge was a long way below.

"He fell?" I asked.

Dan smirked. "Or he was pushed. Either way—he landed with a deadly splat on the rocks!"

I backed

away from the railing.

It wasn't sturdy after years of

neglect. I wondered what had

become of the other kid. The

one who did the pushing.

"Eddie claimed Mark fell," Dan said. "There were **NO WITNESSES**, so Eddie got away with it."

"Is Eddie still around?" I asked.

Dan shook his head.

"He died last month. Mark's parents left the house a long time ago," Dan said. "They were **TOO SAD** to stay here."

Dan looked over the railing. The wind blew his hair back.

I heard him let out a very scared "YIKES!"

Dan's face was PALE when he turned to me. He looked SHOCKED. "I'm going home," he said. "There's nothing here but dust."

"Wait!" I said. But Dan rushed down the stairs.

I leaned over the railing to see what had scared him. All I saw was the rocky creek.

The wind grew stronger. It made a whistling *ooooooh* as it swirled in the gorge. Was that what I'd heard last night?

The *ooooooh* turned to a terrified **AAAAAAH!** It sounded like someone screaming.

I heard a sickening *splat* on the rocks below. But when I looked that way, all seemed calm. The *oooooh-ing* returned. Closer.

I *RAN* all the way home again.

Chapter 3

Help!

I felt like a coward for running from the house. I shouldn't have been AFRAID in the daylight.

I did some research, typing the name of our town and *DAVIDSON MURDER*. A website said Mark Davidson had died by falling from a deck. A CRIME was suspected, but never proven.

The date SHOCKED me. Mark

had died exactly sixty years ago toda

Stuuuuuuu...

Dan refused to return with me that night. He wouldn't say why, but I knew he'd been **SCARED** by something he'd seen.

I decided to go at midnight. But I heard that *eerie* voice calling my name soon after the sun set.

I waited until

after 10:00 p.m. Then

I quietly left our house.

The night was **cold** but clear.

I had to force myself to go upstairs. Every step creaked. The wind MOANED.

I didn't belong here. I was alone, but it didn't feel that way. I felt as if someone were *watching* me.

33

A sharp cry for help
seemed to CUT through me.
I hurried to the railing and
looked down.

Mark was swinging from a tree branch above the gorge. He was SCREAMING my name. *How did he know me?* I tossed the rope and held on. There was a slight tugging at the end of the rope. Mark was climbing up!

Suddenly I was FACE-TO-FACE with a ghost. "Why were you down there?" I asked.

Mark's FACE turned a deadly red. "Because he keeps pushing me over the railing!" he said.

"Who keeps pushing you?" I asked. It didn't make sense. Mark was already DEAD!

Mark reached for my arm. His fingers felt like **spider webs**. "Him," he said, pointing toward the corner. "My *murderer!*"

I turned to look, and I felt the
coldest chill of my life.

Chapter 4
Watch Out!

The other ghost VANISHED.

"Why is he pushing you?" I asked.

"To keep me from telling you that he killed me," Mark said. "Now Eddie wants to kill you, too!"

I GULPED. "Why me?"

"Because you can hear and see me. You know the **TRUTH**. For sixty years, no one heard my *CRIES*," Mark said. "You can let it be known that Eddie was a *murderer*."

"I thought Eddie was a kid."

"He was when he killed me," Mark said. "But he got to grow up. I didn't."

Eddie's ghost reappeared.

He soared toward us.

"WATCH OUT!" Mark yelled.

I ducked as the older ghost flew into Mark, shoving him over the railing. The ghost had superstrength. Suddenly I was FALLING, too!

Tree branches

SCRATCHED

my face, and I

grabbed tight with

both hands. The tree

stopped my fall. I was

dangling high above the

GORGE.

I took a **DEEP** breath and began to climb down. Very carefully!

I reached the lowest branch. It was still a long drop to the GORGE, but I was right above a pool of water.

"It's DEEP," Mark called. "You'll survive. Just let go and stay clear of the rocks."

My hands were
shaking. I took a deep
breath and braced for
an icy soaking.

As I crawled out of the water,
I was cold, wet, and scared to death.
But I was ALIVe.

And I had an important message
to pass on.